FAIRY TALE
SEQUELS

I0540812

BOOK 1

The Three Little
Pigs

Selected Books by Jan Yager

Children's Books
(Illustrated by Mitzi Lyman)
The Cantaloupe Cat
The Reading Rabbit
The quiet Dog

Fiction/Poetry/Creative Writing
Fairy Tale Sequels,
Book 1 – Little Red Riding Hood
A Week with Mom: A One-Act Play
On the Run (a novel)
The Pretty One (a novel)
Untimely Death (a novel) (with Fred Yager)
Just Your Everyday People (a novel) (with Fred Yager)
In Love and Work: Poems (with Fred Yager)

Nonfiction
When Friendship Hurts
Road Signs on Life's Journey
365 daily Affirmations for Happiness
1001 Affirmations
How to Finish Everything You Start
Help Yourself Now
Work Less, Do More: The 7-Day Productivity Makeover
Friendgevity

FAIRY TALE SEQUELS

BOOK II

The Three Little Pigs

Jan Yager

Hannacroix Creek Books, Inc.
Stamford, Connecticut

The author wishes to acknowledge, with gratitude, the helpful
suggestions for the sequel part of this book by her husband,
author Fred Yager.

ISBN: 978-1-938998-84-3 (trade paperback)
An E-book version is also available

Table of Contents

A Note to Parents or Educators

This is Book 2 in my *Fairy Tale Sequels* series. It includes a retelling of a classic fable or folk tale of "The Three Little Pigs" as well as my original sequel followed by activities you can engage in, references and a list of children's books and related media.

This series was inspired decades ago when I would tell a fairy tale or a fable to my firstborn son Scott, who was then three years old, and he would not want the story to end. I found myself making up sequels to each of the classic stories, and those sequels seem to provide as much enjoyment for Scott as the original tales.

This book is set up so that if you, or the child you are reading the classic fairy tale or fable to, and the sequel, want to make up your own sequel, you are encouraged to do so in Part 3 of this book. If you find yourself creating a sequel with your child, you could consider even tape recording it with your smartphone or a tape recorder, writing it down when you can get to it.

Some parents, educators, or even children will be comfortable about creating an original sequel. That's just fine. Go by your lead on this as well as your child's lead. You may encourage this type of activity by asking questions like, "How would you continue this story?" or "What new adventures might you put the three pigs into?" or "Does the wolf return?"

If a child declines creating his or her own original sequel, hopefully this book will still become a welcome addition to his or her personal library. Also, you might find, in time, a child (or you) become more comfortable creating your own sequel or children, in a classroom or even at a book event at a library, may be more motivated to share a sequel or two. Make sure you emphasize that there is no right or wrong sequel. All versions are welcome.

Book 2 – What's Ahead

Part 1 is an introduction intended for parents, educators, or librarians who might be putting together a "The Three Little Pigs" reading event to read by way of background to this famous tale.

Of special interest to parents, educators, and librarians may be the summary of the 1989 controversial retelling by Jon Scieszka, *The True Story of the 3 Little Pigs!* which went on to sell more than 3 million copies globally. As discussed in Part 1, Scieszka depicts the wolf as a victim rather than the perpetrator. According to this version of the tale, the wolf was only going over to his neighbor pig's house to borrow a cup of sugar when he sneezes and because of that, the first pig's flimsy house is blown down, killing the pig. Since the pig accidentally died, in Scieszka's version of the tale, the wolf figures he might as well eat the pig rather than let the pig go to waste.

This version even led to an intriguing discussion by Sara Rowley which was edited by The Janet Prindle Institute for Ethics. It is entitled "Guidelines for Philosophical Discussion, The True Story of the Three Little Pigs by Jon Scieszka," and it is posted online at the Prindle Institute for Ethics in 2020. In that analysis, the plot of Scieszka's version of the classic fable is used to make a comparison to what happens when someone is wrongly accused of a crime that was really an accident.

Part 1 also discusses what I see as the strengths of "The Three Little Pigs" including the famous repeated lines, "Not by the hair on my chinny chin chin!" and the wolf's repeated response, "Then I'll huff, and I'll puff, and I'll blow your house in."

There is also a discussion of the messages in several of the classic versions of the tale.

Parts 2 and 3 are for children of all ages, consisting of the retelling of the classic fable, followed by this author's sequel.

Part 4 is Activities and More including references. The activities may be completed by children, but teens and adults may find the activities fun to do with the questions that are posed entertaining to answer.

References are divided into two parts. The first part is for works cited in this book and further references. The second is a list of additional children's books and related media listings including several versions of "The Three Little Pigs."

Thanks for reading *Fairy Tale Sequels, Book 2, "The Three Little Pigs."* I hope you find it informative and entertaining.

Jan Yager, Ph.D.
https://www.drjanyager.com

Part 1

The Origins of "The Three Little Pigs" and the Tale's Evolution*

It is challenging to pinpoint where, when, and how the classic fable "The Three Little Pigs" originated. There is reference to a "little piggy" in the original Mother Goose rhymes, but it has little resemblance to what would become the classic fable, "The Three Little Pigs."

> This little piggy went to market,
> This little piggy stayed home,
> This little piggy had roast beef,
> This little piggy had none.
> This little piggy went …
>
> Wee, wee, wee,
> all the way home!

According to folklore expert Professor D.L. Ashliman, professor emeritus from the University of Pittsburgh, the earliest origin seems to be a fable called "The Fox and the Pixies" which was published anonymously in Dartmoor, an area in southern Devon, England, in the 1853 book entitled *English Forests and Forest Trees: Legendary, and Descriptive.* The characters in this fable are a fox, not a wolf, and pixies, not pigs. But there are similar themes and even language to what would become the classic "The Three Little Pigs" fable as the fox asks to enter the pixie's house. The fox says, "Let me in, let me in."

In this version, the fox gets into the first and second houses and eats both pixies.

The third house is "an iron house" and the fox cannot get into it. The rest of the story describes how the fox tries to trick the pixy by offering turnips and that they should go to a fair together.

In both cases, the pixie outfoxes the fox.

Then there is a third and final confrontation between the fox and the pixie. Initially it looks like the pixie will be dominated by the fox, but the pixie prevails when the fox falls for the pixie's lure, "Let me out." Said the pixy, "and I will tell you a wonderful secret."

In this version, the fox falls for this and the pixie locks the fox in a box "and there at least he died."

As you probably know, over the years, the fable of "The Three Little Pigs" had endings where the first two pigs are eaten and then the wolf is killed or where the pigs can run away, and the wolf runs away as well.

The first printed version of "The Three Little Pigs" that most of us know can be traced to *Nursery Rhymes and Nursery Tales* by James Halliwell published in 1842. (As with "Little Red Riding Hood," it has been said that the story of "The Three Little Pigs" was shared through an oral tradition.) Halliwell, born in London, was a

British Shakespearean scholar but he is known today for his printed collection of folk tales and nursery rhymes.

Another version of "The Three Little Pigs" that is even more like the one we all are most likely to remember was written by Joseph Jacobs. Australian-born Joseph Jacobs (1854-1916), who also studied anthropology, became known as one of the foremost experts on fables and folktales. "The Three Little Pigs" is contained in one of his many books including *English Fairy Tales* (1890), *More English Fairy Tales* (1893). From 1899 to 1900, Jacobs was also editor of the journal *Folklore* of The Folklore Society.

In 1906, Andrew Lang, who was born in Scotland, included "The Three Little Pigs" in one of his many volumes. This one, published in 1892, was entitled, *The Green Fairy Book.* (It was preceded by *The Blue Fairy Book,* published in 1889, and *The Red Fairy Book,* published in 1890.

Over the years, the fable of "The Three Little Pigs" has been retold and shared in written form but it was not till 1989, when the dramatic rewriting of the classic fable. "The Three Little Pigs," discussed below, takes a dramatic turn.

Most of the written or dramatic versions of "The Three Little Pigs" follow similar plot lines. The key difference is whether the pigs are killed by the wolf and what happens at the end of the story to the wolf.

The Walt Discney 8 minute animated film, "The Three Little Pigs," which was released on May 27th, 1933, was a blockbuster not without its controversies. As cinema historian Michael Lyons shares in his blog, "Big Bad Blockbuster: The 90th Anniversary of Disney's 'Three Little Pigs,'" posted at the Cartoon research website, cartoonresearch.com, "The Disney story team removed the fable's darker elements focusing on the titular characters, the Fifer Pig, who plays the flute, the Fiddler Pig, who fiddles the day away, and the Practical Pig, who is focused on building a sturdy house of brick to protect him when the Wolf comes to the door."

Lyons shares that the cartoon was so successful that it was held over in theaters for weeks beyond its original run. Costing $22,000 to produce, according to Lyons, it grossed

$250,000, and won the Oscar for Best animated Short Film.

The song in the animated short, "Who's Afraid of the Big Bad Wolf," written by Frank Churchill and Ted Sears, according to Lyons, "became an anthem during the depression, at a time when everyone felt 'the Wolf,' in so many ways, was at their door.'"

The controversial part of the short was that originally there was a scene where "the Wolf as a caricature of a Jewish peddler attempting to get into the pigs' houses" led to that version being removed "when the short was re-issued in 1948." Continues Lyons, "The sequence was changed to feature the wolf as a less ethnic" …salesman.

A more contemporary popular version of "The Three Little Pigs" was developed when it became one of the episodes of the live action drama series known as Faerie Tale Theatre. It started in 1982 and ran for six seasons. The episode entitled "The Three Little Pigs" aired on February 12, 1985, and it starred Billy Crystal, Jeff Goldblum, and Valerie Perrine.

The episodes were continually repeated because when he was two and three years old, my son Scott absolutely loved that show! We rewatched it frequently. (As most parents or caregivers know, when a child loves a particular show, they often want to watch it repeatedly.)

So, when Scott was four and my husband Fred and I were deciding what we would name Scott's younger brother who was due to be born in early

1990, we asked Scott if he had a suggestion.

Without hesitation, he proposed naming his new brother *Jeff* since Jeff Goldblum was his favorite actor in the Faerie Tale Theatre production of "The Three Little Pigs."

So, this fable and the messages that it shares – to listen to your parents and to put in hard work and not take the easy way out – has special meaning for me and my family! (Yes, we named our second son *Jeffrey*, although he prefers to be known by the shortened version, his brother's original suggestion, *Jeff*.)

In 1989, a book I have mentioned before would be published that would become a huge bestseller, forever changing the way some people look at "The Three Little Pigs" fable. It was written by a teacher by the name of

Jon Scieszka and it was illustrated by Lane Smith. That 32-page book was called *The True Story of the 3 Little Pigs!*

According to the author's website, jonscieszka.com, since it was published, that book has sold more than 3 million copies around the world, and it has been translated into 14 languages.

Here, in a nutshell, is the plot of this unique retelling of the age-old folktale. The author cleverly lists on the cover that the book is written by "A. Wolf" "As told to Jon Scieszka." The author has the wolf writing his version of the tale in the first person, stating on page 2, ""' I'm the wolf. Alexander T. Wolf. You can call me Al."

As mentioned previously in the "A Note to Parents and Educators" in this book, according to Jon Scieszka's parody, the wolf was a neighbor to the three pigs. In this parody told by the wolf, the wolf just needed to borrow a cup of sugar because he was baking a birthday cake for his grandmother. But when he went over to the first pig's house, he sneezed and that blew the house down, killing the pig. Since the pig was dead accidentally, according to Scieszka's version, the wolf figured it might as well eat the pig since he was hungry. The second to last page of this version, concludes, "That's it. The real story. I was framed."

The book, labeled a children's book with the publisher listing on the back cover that it is for "Ages 3-8," although teens and adults might be more inclined to appreciate its controversial approach to the classic fable, then shows how the wolf was really the victim of a series of accidents and misunderstandings. Bestselling author James Patterson even considers this version of the three little pigs important enough to highlight it at his website, jamespatterson.com.

At Jon Scieszka's his website, the former teacher, in the section entitled, "Educators," in the subsection, "Twisting Fairy Tales and Fables," in the part related to his book, *The True Story of the 3 Little Pigs,* suggests:

- "Have your own courtroom trial.
- Tell any story from a different point of view.

- Learn about an "unreliable narrator"."

Another controversial version of the age-old fable is the 1993 book by Eugene Trivizas, *The Three Little Wolves and the Big Bad Pig*. Illustrated by Helen Oxenbury, this approach is to make the wolves the victims and the pig the villain or perpetrator. (On the back cover, the publisher lists the age group for this version as Ages 7-10).

If you read the very first page of this revised version of the classic fable, you will see how it edits the original story as the mother tells her three little wolves, who are asked to go out into the world, "Go and build a house for yourselves. But beware of the big bad pig."

This is a dramatically different "take" on "The Three Little Pigs story in so many ways. The obvious one is that it is about a big bad pig and three wolves, not three little pigs. But the differences go beyond that since in this unique version, you will find the three wolves live together, and the first version of their house is a brick one, but the pig still can destroy it. The pig even destroys the next two versions which are made even stronger.

What kind of house the three wolves make that does not get destroyed by the "big bad pig" is truly a surprise, as is the upbeat, positive ending.

Messages and Repetition

One of the strengths of this age-old tale is that there are strong messages to it:

1. Listen to your parents' advice. If your mother says you need a strong house, she probably knows what she's talking about.

2. Don't take the easy way out and build a straw or stick house because it may not withstand more powerful intruders.

3. Hard work pays off like the third pig's sturdy house of brick that withstood the wolf.

Repetition, mentioned previously, distinguishes this classic fable with the "Not by the hair of my chinny chin chin" and "then I'll huff, and I'll puff, and I'll blow your house in." Even the unique version by Eugene Trivizas rewritten with three little wolves and a big bad pig rewrites that most famous of all lines from the classic fable: "'No, no, no,' said the three little wolves. 'By the hair on our chinny-chin-chins, we will not let you in…" Adding this phrase unique to this rewritten version "…not for all the tea leaves in our china teapot!;"

In addition to the repeated phrases in the classic tale, and even in the different version by Eugene Trivizas, the fact that there are three pigs,--Trivizas has three wolves-- not just one or even two.

This is known as "the power of three." The great Roman orator, lawyer, and writer, Cicero, is associated with this Latin phrase, "*omne trium perfectum*" which means "everything that comes in threes is perfect."

Another strength of the classic fable is how it can inspire a discussion about stereotypes. As you will see from the list of ten factors about pigs compiled by Julie Cappiello, pigs are not dirty or dumb.

10 Details About Pigs

I want to conclude this first part of *Fairy Tale Sequels, Book 2, "The Three Little Pigs"* with 10 fun facts about pigs gleaned from the article by Julie Cappiello posted at the World Animal Protection website (www.worldanimalprotection.us):

1 Pigs are clean animals.

2. Pigs are unable to sweat.

3. According to Cappiello's research, pigs are smarter than dogs.

4. Mother pigs sing to their piglets (babies).

5. A favorite of pigs is having their bellies rubbed.

6. Another trait is that pigs have an exceptional sense of direction.

7. Pigs like to sleep nose-to-nose and pigs' dream.

8. An outstanding memory is another trait of a pig.

9. "Pigs suffer immensely on factory farms."

10. "Pigs are deserving of good lives."

Now on to the classic "The Three Little Pigs" folktale, followed by my sequel, that has captivated so many of us for hundreds of years!

Part 2

A Retelling of the Classic Fable of "The Three Little Pigs"

Once upon a time, there were three pigs who had grown up with their mom but now that they were old enough, it was time for them to venture out on their own. They all wanted to stay and were reluctant to leave the only home they had known, but Mother Pig, who was finding it hard to keep all three sons fed, knew it was time for them to become more independent.

"Make sure you build a sturdy enough house for yourselves," advised Mom Pig.

She quickly added, "And watch out for any wolves."

They agreed and all three of her pigs went merrily on their way.

But the first pig was a lazy pig. He just wanted to play all day. So, he gathered straw that was readily available, and he quickly made a straw house so he could relax and play the fiddle.

The second pig was more cautious and hardworking. He made his house of sticks. It took longer to build his house, but his wood house was still not a very sturdy house. Soon, he too was finished so he could put up his feet and relax inside his new home.

The third pig was the most diligent and hardworking pig of the three brothers. He knew there was a hungry wolf nearby, so he built his house of bricks even though it took longer. He built his house, brick by brick.

It took three times as long to finish his house of brick as his brothers'

houses of straw and sticks. But the third little pig's house was a much stronger house.

Soon, after the third pig finished his house, a wolf came down the mountain. He went to the first house of straw and knocked on the door.

"Little pig, little pig, let me in," said the wolf as he licked his lips at the thought of tasting the pig.

"Not by the hair of my chinny chin chin," said the first pig.

"Then I'll huff, and I'll puff, and I'll blow your house in," cried the wolf.

Just then, the wolf began to blow down the house, which came down very quickly.

As the straw house fell, the first pig ran out the back door, and to his second brother's house made of sticks.

"I'm safe," said the pig as he sank into a comfortable chair in his second brother's house.

Just then, there was a knock at the door,

"Little pig, little pig, let me come in," said the wolf as he licked his lips again at the thought of tasting the two pigs.

"Not by the hair of my chinny chin chin," said the second pig.

"Then I'll huff, and I'll puff, and I'll blow your house in," cried the wolf.

Just then, the wolf began to blow down the wooden house of sticks. But the two brother pigs ran out the back door of the wood house just as it came tumbling down.

They ran to the house of their hardworking third brother.

"Our mother told you both to build a sturdy house," said the third brother. "But I will let you both in because you are my brothers."

Just then, the three pigs heard a knock at the door.

"Little pig, little pig, let me come in," said the hungry wolf as he licked his lips at the thought of eating all three pigs.

"Not by the hair of my chinny chin chin," said the third pig.

"Then I'll huff, and I'll puff, and I'll blow your house in," cried the wolf.

Just then, the wolf began to huff and puff, but he could not blow down the brick house. So, he took a very deep breath, and he tried again and again. But the sturdy house built of bricks did not come down.

So, the hungry wolf got another idea. Now he climbed up to the top of the brick house and started to come down the chimney.

But the hardworking third pig heard the wolf on the roof, and he screamed up to him, "There is boiling water on the stove to greet you if you come all the way down the chimney."

But the wolf came down the chimney anyway, landing in the pot of boiling water. However, he jumped out of the pot as fast as he could and ran out of the house, never to be seen again.

The End

(Or is it the end?)

Part 3

"The Three

Little Pigs"

— A Sequel

What follows is this author's sequel to the classic fable. Thanks for sharing this suggested sequel and, if the spirit moves you, thanks for creating your own sequel and encouraging children to do the same.

Sequel to "The Three Little Pigs"

by Jan Yager

Now that the wolf had run away, the third pig asked his brothers, "Will you now both build stronger houses?"

"Oh no," said the first pig. "The wolf will never come back again, and I want to play my fiddle."

So, the first pig went back to where his house had been. He cleared the straw off the ground and even used the same straw to build another flimsy house.

"Second brother," said the third pig. "Please don't' rebuild your house of sticks. It isn't strong enough and the wolf may come back."

"Oh, older brother," said the second pig. "You worry too much. The wolf will never return."

So, the second brother returned to the pile of sticks that had been his home and he rebuilt his home out of the same sticks and wood.

Fortunately, the third pig still had his house standing, but he decided to make his brick house even stronger. He even fixed the chimney so he would not have to worry about the wolf or any other animal coming down it ever again.

One day, about a week later, when all the brothers were enjoying their homes, there was a rumbling and a grumbling and suddenly they heard the loudest sounds they'd ever heard. Was it a wolf? It sounded much louder than a wolf. Or was it a lion? No, there were no lions where they lived.

What was it?

It turned out to be a big, brown grizzly bear.

The bear smelled that there was a pig nearby and his nose led him to the site of the first pig's house.

"Little pig, little pig, let me come in," said the bear.

"Not by the hair of my chinny chin chin," said the first little pig.

"Then I'll kick down the door," said the bear.

On the count of three, the giant bear pushed in the straw house as the first pig ran out the back door.

The bear quickly went to the second house made of wood.

The second pig looked out his window. His ears were quivering with fright.

"Let me in," said the bear.

"Not by the hair of my chinny chin chin," said the second little pig.

So, the bear swung his strong arms at the door and pushed it in so he could get into the not-too-sturdy house made of sticks as the second pig ran out the back door.

Now the big grizzly bear went to the third house.

"Little pig, little pig, let me in," the bear said.

"Not by the hair of my chinny chin chin," said the third pig.

The third pig locked the front door. He was not afraid of the bear. He stood there, confident, because he knew the bear could not get into his house made of bricks.

The bear swung at the door, but nothing happened except the bear hurt its paws.

The bear tried hitting the door again, and then the walls of the brick house, and even the windows, that were made of very sturdy and unbreakable glass, but nothing happened.

No matter how hard the grizzly bear tried, the house made of bricks was safe from the bear's angry hits.

The two younger brothers who had taken refuge in their brother's brick house hid behind him, afraid of the bear's enraged strikes.

But their older brother was calm and confident since he knew his house of bricks could withstand the bear's attack.

"I have an idea," said the third pig as he went to one of the cupboards in his sturdy home.

He opened the cupboard and removed a big jar of honey. But as he walked toward the front door, his two brothers got nervous.

"What are you going to do?" asked the first pig.

"Yes, we're scared," said the second brother.

"Look out the window," said the third brother pig. "Where is the bear?"

"The bear is sitting under a tree licking its wounds from trying to break down your door," said the second pig.

"Good. I'm going to open the door very briefly and put this honey outside the door."

"No!" shouted the first pig.

"Please don't." shouted the second pig.

"You keep your eye on the bear. If the bear is under that far away tree, we'll be okay."

So, he opened the door and quickly placed the big jar of honey in front of it. He then quickly closed the door and locked it.

Within a few moments, the bear stood up from the far away tree, sniffed into the air, and went over to the jar of honey.

The bear opened the jar and took out a big portion of honey with his fingers, licking the honey off his hand. It tasted delicious! This bear, like most bears, loved honey!

After eating a few more portions of the honey, the bear was on its way into the woods.

"Thank you for saving us," said the first pig to his brother. "I'll find a way to build a sturdier house this time."

"Yes, big brother. I'm going to go back to my pile of wood and make my house again, but I will make it stronger this time as well."

The third brother considered their options and after a several moments he said, "I have another idea. Why don't we make this brick house bigger so all three of us can live together till we find another pig we want to live with and settle down with. That way we'll all be safe from wolves and bears as we live together in a sturdy house made of brick."

"And let's add some devices like a wolf or bear detector to our home that will make it a smart home, like us." said the second pig.

"And let's make sure we seal up the chimney so a wolf or any other animal can never go down it again," said the first pig.

The brothers agreed and within a few weeks they had finished expanding and improving their sturdy brick house.

They had some adjusting to do since they had all been living alone before. The third pig had to become more accepting of the differences among all three of them. The first pig agreed to only play his fiddle for thirty minutes a day when his brothers were busy or out of the house. The second pig agreed to help with all the chores that needed to be done in their smart home. Despite the adjustments they had to make so they could live together in harmony, they liked being around each other again as they had during their earliest years.

Their first guest to their expanded smart brick home was Mother pig who was so proud of her three pigs.

"I knew you pigs would find a way to make it on your own," she said.

The three little pigs also made sure they always had ample jars of honey available just in case they were again visited by a hungry grizzly bear.

The End

Part 4

Activities and More

This part of this book includes activities for readers to complete as well as references for further reading or viewings.

Activities for Readers

1. Discuss the original fable of "The Three Little Pigs." What are some of the ideas that you learned from the classic retelling of "The Three Little Pigs" that you found especially interesting and useful?

Here are some ideas to consider from the classic tale:

- If your parents issue a warning to you, consider heeding it.
- By building a studier house that could withstand the wolf the third pig saved the day.
- Working hard and smart leads to rewards.

2. What about ideas related to the sequel/

- Just because the wolf was no longer a threat does not mean there are not other aggressive animals to deal with.

- The third pig decided to use the honey to appease the bear.

- Deciding to work together to build a bigger smart house was a way for the three pigs to help each other.

- Instead of living alone, living together may require adjustments but it also offers benefits.

- The actions the three pigs took showed their mother that they had taken her warnings seriously and had succeeded.

2. Why do you think the story of "The Three Little Pigs" is so timeless?

3. Have you ever been tempted to be like the first pig, wanting to play all day instead of doing the required hard work? If yes, when did that happen and what did that experience teach you?

4. Compare the original retold fable to the sequel that you just read or had read to you. What are the similarities between the two versions of The Three Little Pigs? What are the differences?

5. There are several children's books that take an alternative approach to "The Three Little Pigs" fable. *The True Story of the Three Little Pigs* and *The Three Little Wolves and the Big Bad Pig* retell the story either from the wolf's point of view

or substitute wolves for pigs and making the villain a pig. If you read one or both popular books, what do you like or dislike about these versions?

2. Writing in Response to Prompts

Here are some writing prompts to help you write a summary or reaction to the two versions of "The Three Little Pigs" that you read in this book:

Writing Prompts Retelling of the Classic Fable

Prompt #1

The mother warns her three pig children: _____

Prompt #2

The first pig likes to play all day and builds a house of _____

Prompt #3

The second pig builds his house of
_____. When the wolf
appears, the house of wood

_____

Prompt #4

The hardworking third pig builds his
house of _____. When the
wolf comes to the third house,

_____

**Writing Prompt Related to the
Sequel**

- The stereotypes about pigs that
  the sequel takes on are

  _____

- "I think the third pig was clever
  to put the jar of honey outside

the door for the grizzly bear because" _____

_____

- "I wonder what it is going to be like with all three brothers living together because they are so different. This is what I think it may be like:" _____

_____

3 Write Your Own Sequel

Now it is time for you to take out a piece of paper, or to work on your computer or tablet, or even using your smartphone, as you write your own sequel to The Three Little Pigs.

Here are some questions to get you started:

How does your sequel begin?

What happens in the middle of your sequel?

How does your sequel end? (If you have purchased this book, you can write your sequel down here.)

_____

_____

_____

_____

_____

_____

_____

_____

_____

_____

3. Draw a picture

For the next activity related to this classic fable, take out a piece of paper, or use your tablet, to draw your own picture associated with either the original fairy tale or the sequel, or even to your own sequel. (If you have purchased this book, you could use this page to make your drawing.)

4. The use of repetition is one of the reasons "the Three Little Pigs" is such a favorite fable. Who can forget these repeated phrases:

"Not by the hair of my chinny chin chin"

or

"Then I'll huff, and I'll puff, and I'll blow your house in."

Can you recall other fables or fairy tales that use repetition in the same way? If yes, please share those repeated phrases.

You might also make up your own phrases that can be repeated.

6. Messages

Another reason "The Three Little Pigs" has stood the test of time are its various timeless messages.

Write down one or more of those messages, in your own words:

1. _____

_____

2. _____

_____

Now write down your own messages for the classic or sequel tales you have read in this book and/or the ones you created:

1. _____

_____

2. _____

_____

3. _____

Works Cited, References, and Additional Children's Books

Bradley, Barbara a., Kelli Thomas, and A. Allen Bradley, Jr. "A Home for Three Pigs." National Science Teachers Association, *Science and Children,* October 2019, Volume 57, page 40-48.

Cappiello, Julie. "10 Facts About Pigs." Posted on 08/30/2022 at the World Animal Protection website.

Chookajorn, Thanat. "How to Combat Emerging Artemisinin Resistance: Lessons from "The Three Little Pigs." *PLoS Pathogens,* April 26, 2018, volume 14.

Grimm, Jacob and Wilhelm Grimm. *Children's and Household Tales.* Gottingen, Germany, 1812.

Grimm, Jacob and Grimm, Wilhelm. Translated and edited by Jack Zipes. *The Original Folk and Fairy Tales of the Brothers Grimm: Complete First edition*. Princeton, NJ: Princeton University Press, 2014.

Halliwell, James. *Nursery Rhymes and Nursery Tales,* 1842.

_____. *Popular Rhymes and Nursery Tales*. 4th edition. London: John Russell Smith, 1849.

Jacobs, Joseph. *English Fairy Tales*. Illustrated by John R. Batten. London: David Nutt, 1890.

Joy, Melanie. *Why We Love Dogs, Eat Pigs, and Wear Cows: An Introduction to Carnism*. 10th anniversary edition. Newburyport, MA: Red Wheel/Weiser, 2020, 2010.

Lang, Andrew, editor. *The Green Fairy Book*. London: Longmans, Green and co., 1892 (reissued by Dover, 1965)

Lyons, Michael. "Big Bad Blockbuster: The 90th Anniversary of Disney's 'Three Little Pigs.' Posted on May 26, 2023 at cartoonresearch.com website.

Maeots, Olga Nikolaevna. "The Tale of the Three Little Pigs: The Evolution of a Fairy-Tale Plot in a Twentieth-Century Picture Book." *Children's Readings: Studies in Children's Literature,* 2021, Vol. 19, pages 215-234.

Ness, Mari. "Politics and Fairy Tales: Early Versions of 'The Three Little Pigs." Tor.com, posted on July 19, 2018.

_____. "Questionable Scholars and Rhyming Pigs: J.O. Halliwell-Phillipps; 'The Three Little Pigs." Posted at Tor.com, July 25, 2018.

_____. "Warner Bros. 'Three Merrie and Looney Version of 'the Three Little Pigs,' Posted at Tor.com, August 16, 2018.

Rowley, Sarah. Edited by The Janet Prindle Institute for Ethics. "Guidelines for Philosophical Discussion, The True Story of the Three Little Pigs by Jon Scieszka." Posted online at the Prindle Institute for Ethics, 2020.

Song, Kim. "Conflict Resolution Strategy in a South Korean Middle School Class: Revisiting "The Three Little Pigs." *Peace Research,* November 2—4, volume 36, pages 77-86.

Vilas-Boas, Eric and John Maher. "The 100 Sequences That Shaped Animation from Bugs Bunny to Spike Spiegel to Miles Morales, the History of an Art Form that Continues to Draw Us In." Posted on October 5, 2020, at Vulture.com.

White, E.B. *Charlotte's Web.* New York: HarperCollins, 1952.

Yager, Jan. *Fairy Tale Sequels. Book 1 – Little Red Riding Hood.* Stamford, CT: Hannacroix Creek Books, Inc., 2024.

Yager, Jeff. "My Lucky Hat." (a short story). 2016. Posted online as an e-book at Amazon.com. Audiobook version narrated by Russell D. Bernstein

Zipes, Jack. *The Golden Age of Folk and Fairy Takes: From the Brothers*

Grimm to Andrew Lang, Hackett Publishing Company, 2013.

_____*Grimm Legacies: The Magic Power of the Grimm's' Folk and Fairy Tales*. Princeton, NJ: Princeton University Press, 2016.

_____. "How the Grimm Brothers Saved the Fairy Tale." *Humanities: The Magazine of the National Endowment for the Humanities*, Volume 36, March/April 2015.

_____. *The Irresistible Fairy Tale: The Cultural and Social History of a Genre*. Princeton, NJ: Princeton University Press, 2013.

Additional Children's books and Related Media

Addabbo, Carole. Illustrated by Valentine. *Dina the Deaf Dinosaur* Stamford, CT: Hannacroix Creek Books, Inc., 1999.

Carle, Eric. *The Very Hungry Caterpillar*. World Publishing Company, 1969. (Originally titled *A Week with Willi the Worm*.)

Christelow, *Eileen. Where's the Big Bad Wolf?* Writer and Illustrator. New York: Houghton Mifflin Harcourt, 2002.

Eastman, P.D. *Go, Dog, Go!* New York: Random House, 1961.

Freeman, Don. *Corduroy*. New York: Viking, 1968.

Funk, Josh. *It's Not the Three Little Pigs (It's Not a Fairy Tale)*. Illustrated by Edwardian Taylor. Two Lions, 2022.

Gilbert, Burt, director. *Three Little Pigs*. Walt Disney Productions. Produced by Silly Symphony. 1933. Animated short film, 8 minutes.

Gunderson, Jessica. *No Lie, Pigs (and Their Houses) Can Fly! The Story of the Three Little Pigs as told by the wolf (The Other Side of the Story)*. Illustrated by Cristian Luis Bernardini. Picture Willow Books, 2016.

Johnson, Crocket. *Harold and the Purple Crayon*. New York: HarperCollins, 1955.

Leaf, Munro. Drawings by Robert Lawson. *The Story of Ferdinand,* New York: Grosset & Dunlap, 1936.

Martin, Emily Winfield. *The Wonderful Things You Will Be*. New York: Random House, 2015.

Novak, P.J. *The Book with No Pictures*. Rocky Pond Books, 2014.

Piper, Wally. *The Little Engine That Could*. New York: Golden Books, 1930.

Scieszka, Jon. Illustrated by Lane Smith. *The True Story of the 3 Little Pigs!* New York: Viking Books for Young Readers, 1989.

Sendak, Maurice. *Where the Wild Things Are*. New York: HarperCollins, 1963.

Storm, Howard Director. *The Three Little Pigs*. Starring Billy Crystal, Jeff Goldblum, and Valerie Perrine. Faerie Tale Theatre. Episode aired February 12, 1985.

Trivizas, Eugene. *The Three Little Wolves and the Big Bad Pig*. Illustrated by Helen Oxenbury. London: Heinemann, 1993.

White, E.B. *Charlotte's Web*. New York: HarperCollins, 1952.

White. E.B. and Earl Hamner Jr., writers. *Charlotte's Web*. Starring Debbie Reynolds, Henry Gibson, and Paul Lynde. Animated. 1 hour 34 minutes. 1973.

Yager, Jan. *The Cantaloupe Cat*. (Illustrated by Mitzi Lyman) Stamford, CT: Hannacroix Creek Books, Inc., 1998. Paperback, 2023.

_____, *Fairy Tale Sequels. Book 1 – Little Red Riding Hood*. Stamford, CT: Hannacroix Creek Books, inc., 2024.

_____. *The Reading Rabbit.* (Illustrated by Mitzi Lyman) Stamford, CT: Hannacroix Creek Books, Inc., 2013.

_____. *The Quiet Dog* (illustrated by Mitzi Lyman) Stamford, CT: Hannacroix Creek Books, Inc., 2013.

Yager, Jeff. Illustrated by Nancy Batra. *Chuck & Alfonzo.* Stamford, CT: Hannacroix Creek Books, Inc., 2020, e-book. Paperback, 2023.

_____ *The Question Is Why?* Illustrated by Nancy Batra. Stamford, CT: Hannacroix Creek Books, Inc., 2016.

About the author

 Jan Yager taught sixth grade school in Philadelphia and later became an Assistant Editor at Macmillan, revising the popular Bank Street Readers. She has a B.A. from Hofstra University. an MA in Criminal Justic from Goddard College Graduate Program, and a Ph.D. in Sociology from CUNY Graduate Center.

Dr. Yager's 60+ award-winning nonfiction and fiction books, translated into 35 languages, include *When Friendship Hurts; Road Signs on Life's Journey; Skills Building Workbook for College Students; How to Finish Everything You Start; Friendgevity;* four novels; and others.

Jan has been teaching college since her mid-twenties, beginning at The New School and, since 2014, in the Sociology Department at John Jay College of Criminal Justice, where she is an Adjunct Associate Professor, among other colleges and universities.

For more on Jan, go to https: www.drjanyager.com.

Other Fairy Tale Sequel Books by Jan Yager You Might Find of Interest

**Fairy Tale Sequels: Book 1
"Little Red Riding Hood"
2024**

**Additional Children's Books
Published by Hannacroix Creek
Books That You Might Enjoy**

Chuck & Alfonzo by Jeff Yager
Illustrated by Nancy Batra
Ages 4-8+
(An excerpt follows)

Chuck rolled over in
his family's
apartment.
in Boston as Nancy
and Bill watched the
news.

"A monkey has escaped from the zoo," the TV reporter exclaimed.

The Question Is Why?

By Jeff Yager

Illustrated by Nancy Batra

Ages 2-6

(An excerpt follows)

"Why do I have to learn the **a**lphabet?"

"Because you need to learn how to read, write, speak and how to sound out words using letters."

"Why do you want me to eat

broccoli?"

"Because broccoli is good for you, and you can't have junk food all the time!"

THE ALPBABET

Based on *The Question Is "Why?"* Written by Jeff Yager Illustrated by Nancy Batra
(Hannacroix Creek Books, Inc., 2016)

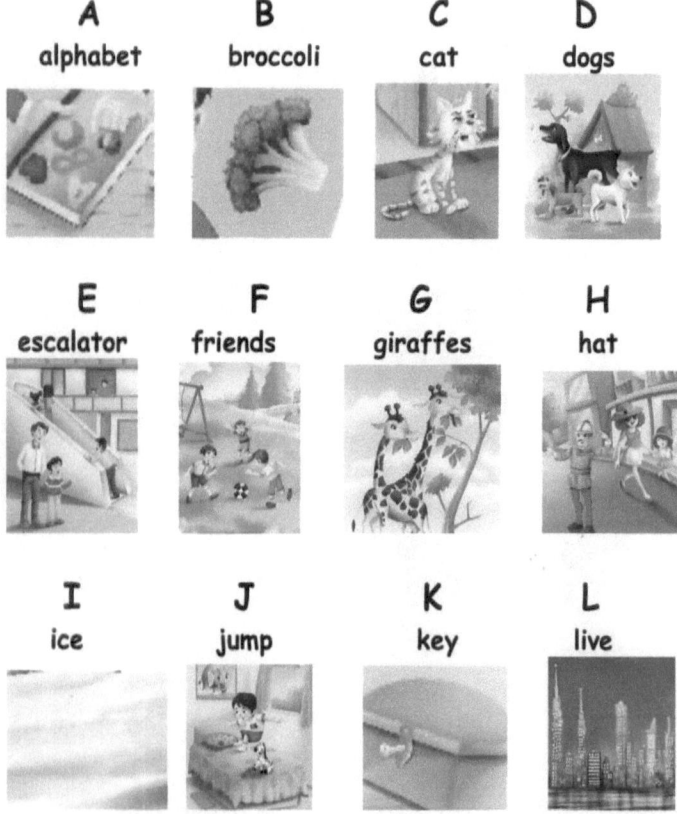

A	B	C	D
alphabet	broccoli	cat	dogs

E	F	G	H
escalator	friends	giraffes	hat

I	J	K	L
ice	jump	key	live

Spanish edition of *THE QUESTION IS WHY?*
A fun way to teach children Spanish!

Suggestion:
Put the Spanish and English language versions of the book, side by side, as children learn how to read and say each sentence in both languages.

Dina the Deaf Dinosaur

Carole Addabbo

Illustrated by Valentine

(An excerpt follows)

Deep in the woods, there lived a mole named Moliere. One day, when he crawled out of his underground tunnel, he found some trash near the tunnel's opening. Moliere rummaged throughe garbage and found an old bicycle without a seat and a sailboat without a sail. He was about to bring these treasures home when he heard a sound.

In a nearby oak tree, there lived a chipmunk named Camilla and an owl named otto. Camilla enjoyed cooking near the window of her tree house where she could watch Otto tinker with an old car. While she was making lunch, she too heard a sound. She checked the kettle, but it was quiet. She looked out the window and heard the sound again.

Age range: Baby through Age 5

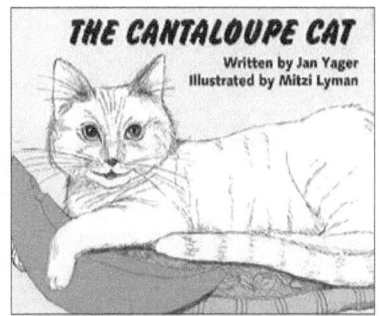

Selected Nonfiction Books by

Jan Yager

How to Self-Publish Your Book Square One Publishers, 2019 English language rights **Foreign translation rights: Hannacroix Creek Books** (e-mail hannacroix@aol.com)

Available in e-book and print formats.

Whether your work is fiction or nonfiction, this book offers step-by-step guidance to help readers to avoid common self-publishing mistakes.

"Leveraging an extensive career in traditional and self-publishing, Yager *(When Friendship Hurts)* offers a comprehensive guide to the latter field, with separate sections on writing one's book, publishing it, and marketing it . . .will prove valuable to anyone seeking to self-publish in a professional manner."— *Publishers Weekly*

How to Promote Your Book
Square One Publishers, 2023
English language rights
Foreign translation rights: Hannacroix Creek Books
(e-mail hannacroix@aol.com)

Available in e-book, print, and audiobook formats.

"Writing a great book is the easy part. Getting people to buy the book is wicked hard. Jan's book shows you what promotion to do so you increase the possibility that your book becomes a bestseller."

—Jeffrey Fox, bestselling author, *How to Become a Rainmaker*

Whether your book is being released through a commercial publisher or an academic press, or you are self-publishing it, as the author, you can and should play a crucial role in getting your title seen, talked about, and sold.

"[Presents] well-organized sections on the basics of book publicity, both pre- and post-publication. Yager explores self-advocacy techniques crucial for driving sales whether as an independent author or under the wing of a publishing house . . .." — *Library Journal*

How to Finish Everything You Start

Available in e-book, print, and audiobook formats

This practical business book helps readers understand why they're not finishing projects, and what to do about it, including using Dr. Yager's unique F-I-N-I-S-H technique. It also goes beyond a "do this, not that" approach to help you develop a deeper insight into what you should be committing to in the first place! Divided into three parts, Part 1, "Causes," Part 2, "Cures," and Part 3, "Additional Thoughts and a Conclusion," includes a chapter entitled, "The Exception That Proves the Rule: When Failing to Finish is a Good Thing" as well "Summing Up," with pivotal examples and information to help you finish everything you start.

Work Less, Do More
The 7-Day Productivity Makeover
Third edition
Available in e-book, print, and audiobook formats
This revised and updated international hit book covers everything from assessing how productive you are right now, goal setting, prioritizing, to getting over procrastination, perfectionism, poor planning, and pacing, 9 other time wasters, organizing, decluttering, teaching time management to your children and teens, work-life balance, and lots more. Well-written, and filled with anecdotes, examples, self-quizzes and worksheets, Dr. Yager also shares the results of her surveys of more than 250 men and women on their time challenges, strengths, and preferred productivity tools.

1001 Affirmations
This book combines three previous affirmations books: *365 Daily Affirmations for Happiness, 365 Daily affirmations for Time Management,* and *365 Daily Affirmations for Healthy & Nurturing Relationships.* Each book includes 365 affirmations plus an introduction, activities for work or leisure time, references, and/or resources. For this composite volume, the author added, "Positive Affirmations: A New Introduction.".

Sample affirmations:
On happiness
#1 "I am responsible for my own happiness."
#57 "I am in my own fan club."

On time management
#3 "I make each minute count."
#20 "I aim for an excellence that is achievable."

On healthy & nurturing relationships
#1 "I am deserving of healthy and nurturing relationships."

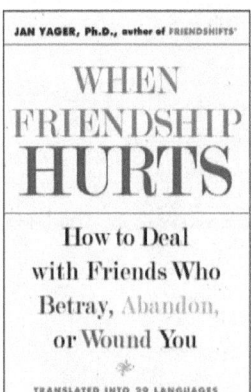

When Friendship Hurts

Simon & Schuster, 2024, 2010, 2002
U.S. and Canada
All other territories,
Hannacroix Creek
Books, Inc.

(hannacroix@aol.com)

We've all had friendships that have gone bad. Whether it takes the form of a simple yet inexplicable estrangement or a devastating betrayal, a failed friendship can make your life miserable, threaten your success at work or school, and even undermine your romantic relationships. Finally, there is help.

In *When Friendship Hurts,* Jan Yager, recognized internationally as a leading expert on friendship, explores what causes friendships to falter and explains how to mend them - or end them. In this straightforward, illuminating book filled with dozens of quizzes and real-life examples, Yager covers all the bases, including:

Friendgevity
2022

In e-book, print, and audiobook formats

This prescriptive self-help book explores how the right friends can extend your life and even delay or avoid the onset of dementia, help with recovery from heart disease, cancer, and other illnesses, and better withstanding of pain. However, the wrong ones -- frenemies and even fatal friends -- can have catastrophic effects. *FRIENDGEVITY* also investigates the impact of social media on friendship.

A goal of *Friendgevity* is to be used as a required or recommended text so students learn more about friendship in Intro Sociology or Psychology courses as well as in Sociology of the Family courses. Appendix IV is "Applying the Four Sociological Theories to Friendship" and Appendix VII is "Critical Thinking Questions." There is also a reading Group Guide for students or Book Club members.

365 Daily affirmations for Healthy & Nurturing Relationships

Audiobook versions narrated by Lindsay Arber.

Positive statements related to key relationships including parent-child, sibling, extended family, friend, romantic partner, neighbors, co-workers, or service providers. Includes an introduction by Dr. Jan Yager as well as activities in the back on how to improve your relationships at work and in your personal life.

Selected Fiction by Jan Yager

**A Week with Mom
A One-Act
Play**

Eighty-one-
year-old
Sandra and
her 56-year-
old married
daughter
Lydia spend a
week together
in London
after Sandra agrees to help staff her
daughter Lydia's table at the London
Book Fair.

Will it be a chance for this mother and
daughter to grow closer, will it be more of
the same, or could there be an even worse
outcome?

www.ingramcontent.com/pod-product-compliance
Lightning Source LLC
Chambersburg PA
CBHW030149200626
46812CB00016B/1756